These poems are shaded in violence and manipulation—but that's what it takes to understand the dynamics of the Manson family. The power of Schwarz's craft is that it slows down, as if sculpting from granite, while also showing a capacious flex of rhythms and ambitions. There's a brightness of approach here, even within the terrible dark of events at hand.

SANDRA BEASLEY, AUTHOR OF *COUNT THE WAVES*

As if we are following the Manson family against our will, *No Name Atkins* is equally dangerous and mystical. Schwarz's deft hand paints these vignettes in masterful, touching, and vivid ways, utilizing language and metaphor to describe what only a few eyes could see. We witness a resurrection of a story that has long fallen out of the public eye.

JOSH DALE, WRITER AND PUBLISHER AT THIRTY WEST PUBLISHING HOUSE

Schwarz has multi-faceted camera of a voice, doing fearless close ups but having the craft to back away when needed to take in the true horror of how Charles Manson dehumanized those in his cult.

CHRISTOPH PAUL, AUTHOR OF *HORROR FILM POEMS* & *AT LEAST I GET YOU < IN MY ART*

NO NAME ATKINS

THE LIFE OF A MANSON FAMILY MEMBER

JERROD SCHWARZ

CL◢SH

Copyright © 2020 by Jerrod Schwarz

Cover by Joel Amat Güell

ISBN: 978-1-944866-70-9

CLASH Books

clashbooks.com

You don't have to prove yourself to me.
You don't even have to prove yourself to you.

SUSAN ATKINS

PROLOGUE: A PLANT ON FIRE, A BOY IN THE DARK

A thousand miles away from baby Susan's cries,
Kathleen Maddox sits outside a government home for boys
in her rusted over Buick–the slow drip and pile of cigarettes
on the parking lot like stalagmites.

Through the building's window, Kathleen watches a guard
shave Charlie's hair down to the scalp–a white and pink blotch
like the skinned over eye of a cave fish.

PROLOGUE: ANATOMY

Susan's sternum congeals; the thorax of a spider.

Inside the house, bottles collide with insects.
The cotton of a child's shirt becomes a sifting pan;
gold beer pulls the marrow of her cracked rib
through to the other side.

Spiders see in fractals, triangles of embedded glass
and *I'm not driving you to a hospital*.

Most baby spiders hatch on their mother's back.

PROLOGUE: THIS ROOM CLOSED FOR REPAIRS

Susan studies the hospital's protocol–a nurse yanks
three IVs and a leaky catheter,
hands a diamond ring to Father.

Her Sunday-blue nails scrape into the room's whitewash.
Brother's *Can we go home?* ebbs beneath her red cuticles,
room 304's sudden drywall.

The nurse's *Jesus Christ, girl!* plunges what is left
of Susan's nails into naked insulation–an active

imagination: bloodline and pink fur
alchemize a pair of wet, clean lungs.

PROLOGUE; CHUCK, CHARLIE, CHARLES

Sweetheart, call me anything.

His fingers skim her scalp, and her curls become waves.
What if I want to give you a new name? He anchors his knee
in between her thighs.

I was technically born No Name Manson,
but you don't want to sleep with a No Name.

She unbuttons her blouse,
tentacles her legs around the backs of his knees
and laughs, *You're right. I don't want to think*
about your parents not loving you.

————————.

Charlie pivots his knee into her crotch,
her skull scrunching against a cheap headboard.
A single *what the hell?* before his fingers
rope around her neck.

Did I say you could know my parents?

and her hands lap at his face.

Okay, okay, how about we both get new names?

and red roots kink into the whites of her eyes.

*I can be Poseidon, and you can be every mermaid
he ever fucked.*

and she feels her throat walls pushed together;
a deeper pair of lips, an eel trapped in coral.

*Do you like your new name? Imagine you're underwater,
imagine my hands are a trident.*

and she passes out. In the dream before she wakes up, a chimera
of every Greek God chases fifty-two eels into an underwater cave.
They fuse into the shape of a woman who escapes
with minor bruises on the neck
and several lacerations below her stomach.

THIRTEEN WAYS TO PAINT JESUS

I.

You blanch the mattress with cheap bleach.
Burnt fibers and streaks of brown blood
melt into pink watercolor.
Chemicals splash and dry into a tin of weed,
replace your teenage lungs
with roommates' laughter; your blushed cheeks.

THIRTEEN WAYS

II.

You hide letters to your brother
in a cigar box, each one stamped
WRONG ADDRESS; your hunt for him
done in secret, your friends' *fuck sympathy*
becomes a communal, black heave.

THIRTEEN WAYS

III.

You topple over with laughter.
Dank air and *The Lone Ranger*
trigger your boyfriend into a charade
of gallops and Native *whoo-whoops!*
You fall onto cracked tile
greasy with beer, with body.

THIRTEEN WAYS

IV.

You let him thrust juvenile,
thrust his excitement into you.
His eyes blink fast; lashes like paint brushes
flinging primary colors
onto your fake smile–cheeks ready
for a rouge like gold-threaded copper.

THIRTEEN WAYS

V.

You pour cups of milk and flour
into a bowl dirty with last night's cake.
A roommate fingers the batter
and says *My friend Chuck
is coming over, he'll love this.*
Your fingers clench the hand mixer.

THIRTEEN WAYS

VI.

His guitar neck leaks through the front door,
your eyes stroke each silver string,
paint bubbles solidifying onto their own oil.
Strong knuckles and tamped callous
burn your roommate's young hands down
to a raw sap when they shake.

THIRTEEN WAYS

VII.

His head drains your eyes of color;
your corneas marbled over
by his hair; one thousand
warped halos. But his smile,
a gritty Beach Boy smile, sculpts you
with ruby irises.

THIRTEEN WAYS

VIII.

His first words, *Hello beautiful,*
slink around your ankles and pull
you down onto the shag carpet.
His banter like silver chains
thread into guitar strings; rebar twisting
your hands into a prayer.

THIRTEEN WAYS

IX.

His southern draw amalgamates
your forced halves–Martha and Mary
– into a face-down Magdalene.
You touch his bare feet, let the strings vibrate
down his toes and into your palm;
an urge to pour out rare perfume.

THIRTEEN WAYS

X.

He bows to the room's ovation
and offers you, Susan, a drink.
Your best *yes, the vodka*
is in the freezer, chokes beneath
his smile; the edges of your mouth
stretch wide with semiprecious dimples.

THIRTEEN WAYS

XI.

He puts on a Beach Boys' record
you thought you knew. Your thin, pale hands
inside his, twenty callous toes
sliding over themselves, shoulders
like mountains rolling into hills
—your soil, his coal, smelted canvases.

THIRTEEN WAYS

XII.

He leaves and you hear the light bulbs
crack, watch the living room paintings
fever up and cook their acrylics
down to splotches of white and silver
and invisible. Your roommates
exfoliate too–skin, then ice.

THIRTEEN WAYS

XIII.

Charles could be your sheets, your fingers
your want; he would be more than happy
to evict your roommates–their tongues
still sizzling acid at twilight.
He could drain your eyes –gold-threaded
copper staining your favorite words;
drug, sleep, hug, brother.

A DRAGON AND A BIRD

The motel maid crumples a bail receipt.

Susan flings her suitcase and herself
into Charlie's VW van. She perches
on the passenger seat, stuffs two pinches of weed
inside two rolls of cigarette paper; hatched eggs in nests.

Charlie claws laughter from her ribs
as she rolls down the window. He whispers hot
in her ear. *I want you in the revolution.*

Susan coughs up *Anything, captain!*
A flap of smoke, a tongue of someone else's fire.

The motel maid flushes the used condoms
down the toilet.

SUSAN BITES HER THUMB

Charlie staples shag carpet to the van's ceiling
while Susan rolls new joints on the dash.
His constant lessons—*the afro-European dynamic
will implode* and *Do you know phrenology?*

Words lull her fingers into perfect scalpels,
shaving green veins, ideal thickness.

A woman walks up to the van; Charlie rolls
his sleeves and flexes his forearms in tandem
with the staple gun's trigger. Her *this is rad!*
and *are you in a band?* stiffen Susan's hands.

Balls of fuzzy leaf spill onto the floorboard
as she crimps the cigarette paper. She licks her thumb
for glue; the woman suggests *maybe we
can meet up in California;*

Susan nibbles the quick beneath her nail
until red spittle ruins her smaller joint.

RAT KING

Charlie's hair is shined leather

when they drive through El Paso. The backseats
are empty, the backseats are covered in cheap blankets
covered in dried sweat from Susan's back and knees.

Charlie's hair is a horse tail

when he says *grab my guitar, sweetheart,* and plays
for the gas station attendant—her blonde hair bobbing
with each new chord.

Charlie's hair is a tumbleweed

when they sleep at the attendant's apartment for the night.
She harmonizes with Charlie's plucking, her high lilt
skipping through *Scarborough Fair.*

Charlie's hair is a bundle of dead rats

when he *says Leslie's going to join us. Viva la Revolution!*

The backseats squeak with the pressure of her duffle-bag
and her legs resting crisscross atop the blankets.

Charlie drives and Susan imagines Tucson, Phoenix, Los Angeles;

imagines his hair becoming dead leaves; imagines dead leaves
floating up above his head and catching on fire;
a halo anyone can touch.

TRADITIONAL MATRYOSHKA DOLLS

usually consist of smaller and smaller wooden children,
but artistic variations exist. En route to California,
an artist is adding the outermost layer of skin:

Tex, who has a gun and shoots stop signs
when the LSD is bunk and the family needs to laugh.

An artist paints the bodies
of the fifth, fourth, third, and second layers:
naked, smiles, raw wood,
color of blank skin.

And the innermost doll? He renames her
Susana and gives her four faces:

a smile for when he trembles
into her thighs,

a frown for when he trembles
into a different person's thighs,

a scowl for when he says
government or *nigger*

and a new expression,
which is anger for love's sake
and splinters and anyone's blood
sopping from those splinters
and *maybe even tears,*
the artist thinks, *because of what will happen*
if she does or doesn't make me happy.

TOUR

Susan follows Charlie and the owner
of Spahn's Ranch. *You said a group of eight?*
Well, you'll have to work, but you can live and eat
for free.

The old cowboy shakes an oak walking stick
at the menagerie of rundown movie sets—alien planet,
Victorian mansion, a cross section of a futuristic submarine.
Susan tiptoes inside the engine room and climbs
scaffolds ending at a sub's command deck.
Her fingers pat cocaine on a defunct sonar screen.
She sneezes out sawdust

and squeals *Fuck, my sinuses!* She fingers the fake buttons
lining the captain's chair, pulls down a working periscope
and scans the California landscape: hills fattening
into small mountains, the ranch's living quarters,

Charlie grabbing the owner's cane and cracking his knee caps.
Susan blinks,

and they are strolling again, Charlie's hands clapping
at whatever the man motions towards. Susan blinks
and Charlie prying the man's jaw off, shouts *bow*
before your new Samson, philistine trash!
as the cowboy's tongue rolls in new angles.

Susan huddles in the captain's chair
and plugs her ears against a swirl of shouts
and whispers *Sugar, where'd you run off to?*
and *just some old cowboy no one will miss*
and *don't you want to see the horses?*
and *this will be our coven, my helter foxhole!*

She wakes up in the van. Someone wipes sweat
from her forehead and coos *poor thing's having*
a bad trip. In the front seat, Tex and Charlie roll joints.

Poor thing.

THE FAMILY'S FIRST STAGE PLAY

Charlie stifles a giggle as the prop knife slides by his ribs;
his scream echoes inside a small, plaster Parthenon.

Three naked girls with NYMPH written on their backs
rush their Caesar, moans mix with more earnest
giggles at his exposed chest, their fingers searching
for his sparse, grey hairs.

Susan hides behind a ceramic copy of Michelangelo's David
and rips off her olive branch tiara.

The other girls are still giggling, her breasts are out,
her fingernails
are dirty, and Charlie starts giggling back.

SCRIMSHAW

She wishes her nails
were osmosis; wishes
she could filter through
chest hair, skin, sinew,
and solidify over his ribs;

to scrawl

a curse onto his marrow:
*only Susan can feel
the stigmata, only Susan
can decipher your prophecy
of apocalypse;*

to sketch her own face
into his sternum: *my eyes
are blinking against
your muscle, Charlie,*

*my ears can hear
who you're holding,*

and my mouth is tight
around your tendons.

CHARLIE TELLS SUSAN: TONIGHT, REMEMBER EVERY DETAIL!

* 4 GRAMS OF PEYOTE

My Susannah, you are eight hundred pounds
of rubber tree, a cork for tonight's fire!

* 9 GRAMS of peyote

My hands have molded a volcano within Los Angeles.
You have to bottle the Saviour's magma with a mind-pen.

* 13 GRAMS of peyote

Yes, Susannah's child-white mind – no nigger blood
or corporate choke – will carve
our war totem!

* 20 GRAMS of peyote

Feel that, my palm
scar? Mama said you fell on a nail, Charlie,

Mamma lied to the new Christ. So bring back

every red truth, my apostle, while I commune

with a host of Bodhisattvas, Pharaohs, and Baal

for their assistance in the love-manifesto of swift steel
and truth.

CAR RIDE THERE

Susan snorts cocaine off the dashboard
and watches the rows of brick and stucco mansions
dissolve into hyacinths.

Tex tosses a box cutter in her lap; she holds her breath
as the handle grows scales, the edge wiggling a forked tongue.

Susan slides her thumb along the weapon's skin
until it draws blood. She chokes a single hiss
from the blade and looks back

outside—similar mansions roll by, their walls fracturing
into piles of dead leaves.

FRONT DOOR

She rings the bell, and the whole house repaints itself
a San Jose cayenne. Her box cutter deforms
into her classmate's dead cat –asleep
underneath Susan's first car.

Another *ding-dong* and the mansion shrinks down
to a single door and her father's suitcases
in the hallway. *I'll send you a check*
every month knocks Susan to her knees–the burn
of old carpet replaces a porch's concrete.

Back on her feet, she clenches the box cutter
or the cat's neck or Dad's first check
until her knuckles are purple,
bangs on the door,
and waits for
anyone to
answer.

SHARON TATE HEARS ELEANOR RIGBY ON THE RADIO

A gaggle of laughter and her curled arms bloody
because *Dear God, please not my baby!*

the words of a sermon that no one will hear

A warm collar drips down her chest.
Her blouse, the whole room dims to red
and black.

in the night when there's nobody there

Her last thought, *not my baby Paul*, drowns
inside her deflated stomach—lacerated skin
and deeper, weaker skin.

the face that she keeps in a jar by the door

THE WHITE CORD

Notice the white rope tied around each of their necks and draped over the high ceiling beam between them. –crime scene description

The white cord around Sharon's neck turns pink – the rope fibers, the carpet fibers, rose petals out of cloth.

Tex's *Suzie, fucking look for money* withers into the other end of the rope – a crushed Adam's apple and a man's skin squeezed blue.

She sits beside the bodies and giggles at the cord's new color. *From red to pink to brown, Tex!*

Charlie, I'll say, we turned them into flowers.

They couldn't plant love roots before us.

Susan fingers a stab wound in Sharon's stomach.

Charlie, we made a forever seed.

CAR RIDE BACK

Brick and stucco mansions oscillate
inside the streetlamp's glow – yesterday's dead leaves
and petals compressed into garage doors, shutters.

Tex tucks a wad of hundred-dollar bills
beneath the driver's seat and tells Susan
Toss the box cutter when we go over that bridge.

She flings her weapon well over the railing
and watches the blade catch moonlight
like iced-over grass in the wind.

Susan cups her ears for the faint *kersplosh*
before curling in a ball to dream

of an armed catfish slicing cattails
and tadpoles in half.

THE DREAMS ARE NOT WHAT SHE EXPECTED

No prison cells made of baby bottles,
no nooses threaded from burning film reel.

Instead, she cleans choir robes with orange sand
and cactus root; the desert around her

is muddy with a fresh rain; Susan scrubs
the smocks down to the color of her skin.

Someone she has never met walks over
and asks *What was she wearing? Was the boy*

crying? The robes become a purple blouse
she could never afford, a sudden wind

becomes the boy's first breath, and Susan's neck
hardens into a crystal: a knock from within

her esophagus, a crack, her shattered throat
and a hand crawling out.

THE FAMILY'S LAST STAGE PLAY

Charlie's slapdash King Arthur wields a rusted scimitar,
wears a brittle crown from a film about Jesus' crucifixion.

Who was supposed to be Merlin?

Susan runs up: bed sheet hanging from her head,
spatula for a wand, blood in the crease of her elbow.

She stood up too fast, and Charlie's *teach me a spell
to kill the dragon!* devolves Spahn's Ranch into masonry,
towers, and parapets of a castle— the family growing
breastplates on their torsos, helmets

over their heads, and Charlie's beard is thicker, and his Beatles shirt
is a minx cape, and a director's chair is a brass throne,
and past the drawbridge and the moat are sigils of a warring faction:

their banners flickering blue then red then blue and Merlin says
*I can't teach you anything. You will save us
from any threat, you will save us from—*

but Arthur is running away, shouting
alien words like *Tex* and *gun* and *fucking cops,*

so Merlin draws alchemic symbols
all over the ground: goat heads and stars
and crescent moons. *Everyone we hate will turn to ash,*

the drawbridge splinters open,

and everyone we love will turn to gold,

the walls are mounted

I will sweep away the kindling,

the knights huddle together

and you will make me a gold promise ring.

FIRST NIGHT IN JAIL (OR HOW TO SPELL WOMB)

Sweat escapes forehead—her detoxing brain
grinds itself like a haphazard stick-shift—and falls
onto cold cement. She curls into the fetal position

and the transmission relaxes; synapses
like wheels roll past her favorite haze—Charlie
seeing Spahn's Ranch for the first time, her breasts
rubbing against a replica saloon's dart board, blood
drying on rugs she could never afford—to the hospital
where she was born.

The sudden, warm fluid of birth startles her more than blindness;
buried sounds, her limbs shrunk and weak.
Her brain pulses eighteen years apart—
a parabola and Charlie's smile
on either end pressing against her whole self.

An adjacent inmate's *shut up, bitch* jams
her cerebellum's axels—parabola and Charlie
and birth and blood drying—with a box cutter
and a gavel, a stiff cot and Susan curled around her own dry skin.

FIRST HEARING (OR A DARK AGES PAINTING)

Susan is still medieval:

courtroom flattened into two dimensions,
judge, lawyer, bailiffs in the foreground and background.
The judge's call to rise splashes like nail polish: everyone
is erased to a sketch.

Arthur's crown is gone, Arthur's scepter
is a toothpick in Charles Manson's mouth,

Merlin self reproduces for 1500 years
until only Susan's genes are left: underweight, sweat,
split ends, eyes dilating.

The judge's words—*no bail* and *will go to trial*—
become illuminated text scrawled on the witness box,

and Susan cannot help but laugh
at the crowd behind her: serfs
with pitchforks and shovels; a cartoon scowl
on each of their faces.

CONFESSION

I.

Susan sits crisscross on the bunk bed
and watches her roommate's eyes zigzag
down the last page of a cheap thriller.

Susan's nose tells Susan's stomach
to digest out of rhythm, to turn bile into cramps
because *when was the last time I snorted anything?*

CONFESSION

II.

Susa does not give her cellmate time
to answer the question. Susan's nose tells Susan's mouth
to theorize that *we are in a box, we are in a cement box*

but there are other kinds of boxes. The roommate closes her book
and Susan's nose forces synaptic energy to her lips. *A box
can be made from wood, and a wood box has three purposes:*

*to hold a baby or to hold treasure or to hold a body
and I know the blueprints for two of these boxes.*

CONFESSION

III.

Susan's nose bypasses Susan's brain,
every axon sizzling towards her mouth:

Both blueprints require a saw no a serrated edge
no a knife no a box cutter yes a box cutter.

Charlie no my Charlie yes my Charlie taught me how to create
two wood boxes in reverse.

First, I dug the box cutter into ribs which keep blood in
and into a placenta which keeps blood out and into more ribs
which are just cartilage and I chewed

the ribs and the blood and the not-yet ribs into a varnish

which is economical no thrifty no natural yes natural and leaves
plenty of the body to fill out the wood boxes.

BELLY (OR LIFE IN PRISON)

Susan cannot stop looking at stomachs:

the bailiff's inside a khaki shirt,
Her lawyer's peeking through a missed button,
and her own stomach beneath an orange jumpsuit.

She turns around; the journalists are scrawling
the judge's verdict on their notepads,
excited lungs pulsing their whole torsos.

Susan closes her eyes and imagines the box cutter
back into her hands, imagines giving everyone's stomach
a sloppy, red smile:

look at the prosecutor cut in half, Charlie

look at the jury box pooling over

with blood, Charlie, and look at the babies

sluicing out of everyone's bellies.

EPILOGUE

I.

Every Friday, Susan volunteers to sweep
the floor of the prison chapel.

When she reaches the pulpit, the whole chapel
begins to melt. She drops her broom,
and the pews are turning into parabolas.

Susan blinks the room grotesque: candles inverting
on themselves, stations of the cross falling into black holes,
the communion cup overflowing with someone's broken bones.

She falls hard on the concrete floor and cracks her hip,
pain forcing her into a blackout, into memory:

Charlie lying with her in bed, telling her
about his stint in jail for theft. *I walked in*
to sweep the kitchen and two inmates
were cutting a third one in half.
They were trying to stuff his body
into the garbage shoot, and I
just kept sweeping. I walk the line,
Susana. I'm on the premise of reality.
You should walk there too.

II.

She wakes up to the lopsided mountain
of her body beneath hospital sheets: *your leg
had to be removed.* The doctor says other words
like *metastasize* and *brain* and *months left.*

The morphine drips, and Susan wonders if Tate's wedding ring
has been rusting inside her body; gold band turning brown
in her stomach, diamond studs scraping against her bones.

More words like *random mutation* and *not because of drugs*
and *cancer either way* become an incantation—the iv bag transmutes
into faces
she can't forget:

the beard she trimmed with scissors,

blonde hair she dyed red then brown,

a news anchor's mouth, *She has been called the devil incarnate.*

Outside her room, guards and camera crews conjure rumors
of a tattoo, Manson's face on her left buttock.

Inside, Susan falls asleep, and puss leaks
through the stitches of her nub.

III.

My hospital room has a window

that has been nailed to its frame,
but that doesn't make the moon
any less real.

In every interview, I say *the drugs turned me
into something I wasn't, something Charlie
could use,* but now I have a morphine drip
and it reminds me of the warmth; a star
draining into my spine, the rest of my body
caught in blue magma.

The night after, Charlie and I took acid
and slept on top of a fake tank
leftover from a war film. *Can you hear
the tread rumbling beneath us, Susana?
You have to promise not to tell anyone
about Tate, okay? You love me, don't you?*

I said *yes* and *yes* and *yes* and Charlie
spent the whole night naming new constellations
in my honor.

A machine pushes more morphine
and the best version of Charlie
appears in the gurney with me:
beard trimmed, shirt washed,
and he's plucking at a guitar.

You love me, don't you?

I look down at what is left of my legs,

my varicose veins, the bracelet on my wrist
that reads *WWJD,* and I know

I should hate him,

but outside the window, it's a cloudless night.
Outside the window, stars push through
the bright lights of the hospital.

My very last *yes*

and he's helping me to that window; his back
is strong again, his hands covered in dirt again
from Spahn's Ranch.

I am bleeding from where the iv came loose,
I can hear the guards calling for the nurses,

but Charlie whispers *it's okay, Susan,*
you never have to hurt anyone,

and a leg grows out of my nub.

We can find a church, we can sing
in the choir every Sunday,

and my hair is long, and my hair is black,
and my waist is thin again,

There's an engagement ring
in my pocket,

and a falling star cuts the window in half,

and I love you, Susan

and the nurses are at the door

and I love you, Susan

and the nurses drag me back to the gurney

and I love you, Susan

and your body is disappearing, Charlie

and I love you, Susan

and I want to go back to the window

and I love you, Susan,

and the nurse pushes her needle. I strain
to point out the window—what's left of Charlie
tracing my name into a cluster of stars.

His transparent lips pursing *Susan*, the nurse
reading my ID bracelet: *Susan,*
and before I faint,
a distant galaxy—*Susan*
exploding against the darkness,
Susan made of light.

ACKNOWLEDGMENTS

To everyone who held these poems in their infancy and grew them, I cannot thank you enough. To Erica for never letting me forget the meter. To AMP for knowing I never needed the pictures. To Jimmy for always seeing the narrative. To Sandra for teaching me that grief (and healing) never exists in a single history.

To family and friends who encouraged me to keep writing, your enthusiasm meant more than you can know. To Adam & Matt for listening to more Charles Manson trivia than you ever cared to learn. To Megan, Ian, Silk, Reese, and Margo for making grad school feel like a family reunion. To Mom, Nan, Pop, Jennie, and Tom for all the ways you spurred me on to create art with compassion. To Briar and Emerson, who are not old enough to read this but remind me daily that empathy and understanding are learned behaviors.

And to Seneca, who loves me through all the indecisions, stresses, and quirks that comes with being partnered to a writer. If this book reaches out and nurses someone, it is only because of your care for all those around you, myself included.

ABOUT THE AUTHOR

Jerrod Schwarz teaches creative writing at the University of Tampa and manages poetry for Driftwood Press. His first chapbook *conjure* was published by Thirty West Publishing House in 2019. His poetry has been featured or published in VICE, New Republic, PANK, Entropy, The Plath Project, and more. He lives in Tampa with his wife and twin toddlers.

ALSO BY CLASH BOOKS

WE PUT THE LIT IN LITERARY

CLASHBOOKS.COM

FOLLOW US

TWITTER

INSTAGRAM

FACEBOOK

@clashbooks